Fast Friends

Two
Stories
by

James Stevenson

Greenwillow
Read-alone

Greenwillow Books

A Division of William Morrow & Company, Inc., New York

Color separations by Harriet Sherman   Design by Ava Weiss

Library of Congress Cataloging in Publication Data
Stevenson, James (date). Fast friends. (Greenwillow read-alone books)
Summary: In the first of two easy-to-read stories a turtle and a snail make
some friends with the help of a skateboard. In the second a mouse and a turtle
learn, through trial and error, how to be friends. [1. Friendship—Fiction.
2. Animals—Fiction. 3. Short stories] I. Title. PZ7.S84748Fas [E]
78-14828   ISBN 0-688-80197-8   ISBN 0-688-84197-X lib. bdg.

JE

CONTENTS

MURRAY
AND FRED

It was a beautiful day
and everybody was playing,
except Murray.
He had nobody to play with.

"Hey," said Murray.

"You want to play and have fun?"

"Not with you, slowpoke,"
 said the rabbit.

"I like to run and jump and stuff."

"Would *you* like to play?" asked Murray.

"Okay," said the squirrel. "I'll meet

you at the top of the maple tree."

"I don't climb trees," said Murray.

"How about on the ground?"

"Maybe later," said the squirrel.

"What's up, fellas?" asked Murray.

"Games, Murray," said a mouse.

"Plenty of action!"

"Can I play, too?" said Murray.

"Sure," said the mice.

"We're racing up to the pond. . . .

On your marks;

get ready;

get set–go!"

Suddenly Murray was all alone.

Murray went home.

"What is it now?" said his mother.

"Nobody wants to play with me,"
said Murray. "They say
I'm too slow."

His mother yawned.

"Have you asked any snails?"
she said.

"Snails?" said Murray.

"Snails are no fun."

He found Fred by a rock.

"Hey, Fred," he said. "Want to play?"

"Are you kidding?" said Fred.

"You know I can't keep up with you."

"I could go slow," said Murray.

"Not slow enough for me," said Fred.

"Don't you find this place
  is awfully lonely?" said Murray.
"You're asking me?" said Fred.
"For two cents, I'd get out of here,
  and go look for some friends."
"Where would you go?" asked Murray.
"I don't know. I'd hit the road
  and take my chances," said Fred.

"I wonder what's out there,"
    said Murray.
"New places, friends, fun,"
    said Fred.
"Maybe I'll give it a whirl,"
    said Murray.

"Mind if I tag along?" asked Fred.

"Well . . ." said Murray.

"You think I'd slow you down,
   don't you?" said Fred.

He sighed.

"Well, have a nice trip," he said.

"You can come," said Murray.

"I can?" said Fred.

"Sure," said Murray.

"Why don't you hop aboard?"

Fred climbed on top of Murray's shell.

"It's nice up here," said Fred.

They set off together.

"Wow," said Fred. "You're really

moving along, Murray."

"You keep a lookout, Fred,"

said Murray. "Tell me

which direction is best."

"Straight ahead and up the hill

looks good," said Fred.

By the end of the day,

the woods were far below.

"Look at the view!" cried Fred.

The sun went down,

and Murray was tired.

"We better call it a day," he said.

"I see a nice place to camp,"

said Fred. "Turn right."

"This place is full of good stuff,
isn't it?" said Fred, looking around.
"That's what's nice about travel,"
said Murray.

Murray found something flat
to sleep on.
"Good night, Fred," he said.
"Good night, Murray," said Fred.

In the morning,

a voice woke them up.

"Hey, what are you doing

on that old skateboard?"

said a mouse.

"Skateboard?" said Murray.

"What skateboard?" said Fred.

"Let's see how good you are,"
said the mouse.
"Here, I'll give you a push."
"Wait," said Murray.
"I've never been on a—"
The skateboard started to roll.

"Hold on, Fred!" shouted Murray.

"Have a nice ride," called the mouse.

"Oh, my goodness!" cried Murray.

The skateboard went faster and faster.

"Steer, Murray!" shouted Fred.

"Steer?" said Murray. "How?"

"I'm going into my shell!" cried Fred
as they raced toward a big tree.

We're going to crash, thought Murray.

At the last moment, he leaned away
from the tree, and the skateboard
went around it.

"Hey, Fred. I think I've learned
how to steer!" called Murray.
"Come out and look!"

Fred peeked out of his shell.

"You're going to hit that rock!" he cried.

"No, I'm not!" shouted Murray. "Watch!"

He leaned to one side,

and the skateboard

went around the rock.

Murray zoomed between two rabbits.

They jumped in the air.

"What was *that*?"

said one of the rabbits.

Murray went around a tree,

and a squirrel fell off a branch.

"Is that *you*, Murray?"

cried the squirrel.

They went through a stream

and scared a fish.

"This is fun!" shouted Fred.

Soon they were almost home.

29

At last the skateboard slowed down
and stopped.

All the animals ran over.

"Gee, Murray, you were really
going fast!" cried a mouse.

"Talk about speed!" said a squirrel.

"I guess we were moving along
   pretty well," said Murray.
"You're the world's fastest turtle,
   Murray," said a mouse.
"What about the world's fastest snail?"
   asked Fred.

"Can we try it, Murray?"

asked a mouse.

"It's sort of dangerous," said Fred,

"for beginners."

"I'll give you a ride," said Murray.

"Get on the back."

"Whee!" said the mouse,

as they started rolling.

"Hold on tight," said Fred,

"and don't rock the board."

They raced down a small hill.

"Thanks, Murray," said the mouse.

"That was great!"

The other animals helped carry
the skateboard back up the hill.
"Can I be next?" asked a rabbit.

Murray took everybody for rides.

When it grew dark, Fred said,

"That's it for today."

"Can we play again tomorrow?"

asked the animals.

"Sure," said Fred and Murray.

Murray pushed Fred home
on the skateboard.
"What a day!" said Fred.
"I'm tired," said Murray.
"All that speeding . . . "
"Now we know what it's like
to go fast," said Fred.
"Yes," said Murray.
"And I can take it or leave it."
"Me too," said Fred.
And they both went
into their shells
and went to sleep.

THOMAS
AND CLEM

Thomas had been hunting
for a nice place to live.
The pond looked perfect.
Thomas had just sat down
when along came a turtle.
"You're new around here,
aren't you?" said the turtle.
"Yes," said Thomas. "Very."

"My name's Clem," said the turtle.

"Where's *your* house?"

"I haven't got one," said Thomas.

"No house?" said Clem.

"What will you do when it rains?"

"Get wet, I guess," said Thomas.

"Like always."

"How will you be able to have
friends over?" asked Clem.
"I don't have any friends,"
said Thomas.
"Tough luck," said Clem.
And he left.

"I guess I need a house,"

said Thomas.

He got to work,

and worked all day.

That night, Clem came back.

"Do you like my house?"

said Thomas.

"Where's the door?" said Clem.

"It's all doors," said Thomas.

"It needs work," said Clem.

Thomas worked even harder

the next day.

In the afternoon, Clem came back.

"Thomas?" he called.

"Where are you?"

"I am in my house," said Thomas,

"and I am looking out my window."

Clem looked inside.

"Empty, isn't it?" he said.

"Want to come in?" asked Thomas.

"No thanks," said Clem,

"I'll wait until it's ready."

"Ready?" said Thomas. "Like what?"

"Oh, you know," said Clem.

"Furniture and things."

"Furniture?"

"Chairs," said Clem. "And a table,
   and on top of the table
   a plate full of cookies."

"Oh," said Thomas.

"Plus milk," said Clem.
   Then Clem left.

The next day, Thomas built
two chairs and a table.
Then he bought some cookies
and milk.

In the afternoon, Clem came by.

"Well, well," he said, sitting down.

"This is downright homey."

He started eating cookies.

Thomas sat down and

ate some cookies, too.

"You know," said Clem,

"this place could use a porch."

"A porch?"

"Sure," said Clem. "So you could

sit there and feel the breeze."

The next morning,

Thomas built a porch.

By the time Clem arrived,

Thomas had put the chairs

out on it.

But Clem just walked

into the house.

"Don't you want to sit

   on the new porch?" asked Thomas.

"Too windy," said Clem.

"Better bring the chairs inside."

"Oh," said Thomas.

   He carried the chairs

   into the house.

Clem sat down.

"Getting low on cookies,"
he said. "In fact, this is
the next-to-the-last one."
He ate it.

"I'll get some more
tomorrow," said Thomas.

"See if they have the fancy
chocolate ones," said Clem,
eating the last cookie.
Then he left.
Thomas watched him go.
Having a friend keeps you
awfully busy, thought Thomas.

When Clem came over the next day,

Thomas was sitting on the porch.

"Hi," said Clem. "Get the cookies?"

"No," said Thomas.

"No?" said Clem.

"No," said Thomas.

Clem looked around.

"What are we going to do

if there are no cookies?"

"Well," said Thomas,

"I thought we could go

to *your* house for a change."

"Impossible," said Clem.

"Why?" asked Thomas.

"Too small," said Clem.

"Where is it?" asked Thomas.

"I'm in it," said Clem.

"You mean–"

"My shell," said Clem.

"That's your house?"

Thomas stared at Clem.

"You told me I had to have
a house so I could invite
friends over."

"Right," said Clem.

"But you don't even have a house,"
   said Thomas.

"No," said Clem, "or any friends,
   either. That's how I know."

"Maybe that's because of the way
you act," said Thomas.
"Now you've hurt my feelings,"
said Clem. "Good-bye!"
He left.

Thomas didn't see Clem the next day,
or the day after that, either.
He bought cookies, and ate them
all alone.

The next day, he walked
around the pond.
Suddenly, he came to a turtle shell.

"Is that you, Clem?" he called.

"Maybe it is, and maybe it isn't,"
said a voice inside the shell.

"What do you want?"

"I got some more cookies,"
said Thomas.
"I've got plenty of cookies
of my own," said Clem.
"Well," said Thomas,
"maybe you'd like to come
sit in my house."
"I've got my own house,"
said Clem.
"Okay," said Thomas.
"See you, Clem."
He started to walk away.

"Wait," said Clem, looking out.

"You want to see something?"

"What?" said Thomas.

"Follow me," said Clem.

Thomas and Clem went

through the tall grass.

"Hey," said Thomas.

"You made yourself a house, Clem!"

"It's not for me," said Clem.

"It's for friends who come over."

"It's nice in here," said Thomas.

"It needs work," said Clem.

"Furniture, and maybe a porch."

"I like it the way it is,"
  said Thomas.

"Cookie?" said Clem.

"Thanks, Clem," said Thomas.